The Birds' Christmas Carol

Kate Douglas Wiggin

Inside Illustrations by John Fernie

AN
APPLE
PAPERBACK

SCHOLASTIC INC.
New York Toronto London Auckland Sydney

ISBN 0-590-42118-2

12 11 10 9 8 7 6 5 4   0 1 2 3/9

Printed in the U.S.A.   42

*To the Three Dearest Children
in the World
Bertha, Lucy, and Horatio*

CONTENTS

I. A Little Snow Bird   7

II. Drooping Wings   12

III. The Bird's Nest   17

IV. "Birds of a Feather Flock Together"   24

V. Some Other Birds Are Taught to Fly   33

VI. "When the Pie Was Opened, The Birds Began to Sing"   47

VII. The Birdling Flies Away   60

I. A Little Snow Bird

It was very early Christmas morning, and in the stillness of the dawn, with the soft snow falling on the housetops, a little child was born in the Bird household.

They had intended to name the baby Lucy, if it was a girl; but they had not expected her on Christmas morning, and a name for a real Christmas baby must be something special — the whole family agreed in that.

Mr. Bird said that he had assisted in naming the three boys — Donald, Paul, and Hugh — and that he should leave the naming of the girl entirely to Mrs. Bird. Donald Junior wanted his sister called "Dorothy," and Paul chose "Luella." But Uncle Jack said that the first girl should always be named for her mother, no matter how hideous the name happened to be.

Grandma said that she would prefer not to take any part in the discussion, and then everybody suddenly remembered that Mrs. Bird had thought of naming the baby Lucy, for Grandma herself — so naturally no one expected Grandma to suggest another name.

Hugh, who until then had been "the baby," sat in one corner and said nothing. There was a newer baby now, and the "first girl," too, — and it made him actually green with jealousy.

But it was too important a matter to be settled until Mamma had been consulted.

Meanwhile Mrs. Bird lay in her room, sleepy and happy with her sweet girl baby by her side. Nurse was downstairs in the kitchen, and the room was dim and quiet. There was a cheerful open fire in the grate; but though the shutters were closed, the side windows that looked out on the church next door were a little open.

Suddenly a sound of music poured out into the bright air and drifted into the chamber. It was the boy-choir singing Christmas anthems. Higher and higher rose the clear, fresh voices, full of hope and cheer, as children's voices always are. Fuller and fuller grew the burst of melody as one glad strain fell upon another in joyful harmony:

"Carol, brothers, carol,
    Carol joyfully,
Carol the good tidings,
    Carol merrily!
And pray a gladsome Christmas
    For all your fellow men:
Carol, brothers, carol,
    Christmas Day again."

One verse followed another, always with the same glad refrain:

"And pray a gladsome Christmas
    For all your fellow men:
Carol, brothers, carol,
    Christmas Day again."

Mrs. Bird thought, as the music floated in upon her gentle sleep, that she had slipped into heaven with her new baby, and that the angels were bidding them welcome. But the tiny bundle by her side stirred a little, and though it was scarcely more than the ruffling of a feather, she awoke.

She opened her eyes and drew the baby closer. She looked like a rose dipped in milk, Mrs. Bird thought, like a pink cherub, with its halo of pale yellow hair, finer than floss silk.

9

"Carol, brothers, carol
Carol, joyfully,
Carol the good tidings,
Carol merrily!"

The voices were brimming over with joy.

"Why, my baby," whispered Mrs. Bird in soft surprise, "I had forgotten what day it was. You are a little Christmas child, and we will name you 'Carol' — mother's little Christmas Carol!"

"What!" said Mr. Bird, coming in softly.

"Why, Donald, don't you think 'Carol' is a sweet name for a Christmas baby? It came to me just a moment ago in the singing, as I was lying here half asleep and half awake."

"I think it is a charming name, dear heart. It sounds just like you, and I hope that, being a girl, this baby has some chance of being as lovely as her mother." At this speech from the baby's papa, Mrs. Bird blushed with happiness.

And so Carol came by her name.

Uncle Jack declared laughingly that it was very strange if a whole family of Birds could not be indulged in a single Carol; and Grandma, who adored the child, thought the name much more appropriate than Lucy.

Perhaps because she was born in holiday time,

Carol was a very happy baby. Of course, she was too tiny to understand the joy of Christmas-tide, but people say there is everything in a good beginning; and she may have breathed in unconsciously the fragrance of evergreens and holiday dinners, while the peals of sleighbells and the laughter of happy children may have fallen upon her baby ears and wakened in them a glad surprise at the merry world she had come to live in.

Her cheeks and lips were as red as holly berries; her hair was for all the world the color of a Christmas candle flame; her eyes were bright as stars; her laugh like a chime of Christmas bells; and her tiny hands forever outstretched in giving.

Such a generous little creature! A spoonful of bread and milk always had to be taken by Mamma or Nurse before Carol could enjoy her supper; whatever bit of cake or sweet found its way into her pretty fingers was straightway broken in half to be shared with Donald, Paul, or Hugh; and when they made believe nibble the morsel, she would clap her hands and crow with delight.

"Why does she do it?" asked Donald, thoughtfully. "None of us boys ever did."

"I hardly know," said Mamma, catching her darling to her heart. "Perhaps because she is a little Christmas child!"

II. Drooping Wings

I̲t̲ ̲w̲a̲s̲ December, ten years later.

Carol had seen nine Christmas trees lighted on her birthdays, one after another; nine times she had helped in the holiday festivities of the household, and for five years, certainly, she had hidden presents for Mamma and Papa in their own bureau drawers.

For five years she had heard " 'Twas the night before Christmas," and hung up a scarlet stocking many sizes too large for her, and pinned a sprig of holly on her little white nightgown, to show Santa Claus that she was "truly" a Christmas child, and dreamed of fur-coated saints and toy-packs and reindeer, and wished everybody a "Merry Christmas" before it was light in the morning, and lent every one of her new toys to the neighbors' children before noon, and eaten turkey and plum pudding, and gone to bed at night in a trance of happiness at the day's pleasures.

Donald was away at college now. Paul and Hugh were great manly fellows, taller than their mother. Papa Bird had gray hairs in his whiskers; and Grandma, God bless her, had been four Christmases in heaven.

But there was another reason why Christmas in the Birds' Nest was not as merry now as it used to be. The little child that had once brought such an added joy to Christmas Day, now lay, month after month, a patient, helpless invalid, in the room where she was born.

Carol had never been very strong in body, and it was with a pang of terror that her mother and father noticed her beginning to limp slightly, soon after she was five years old. She also complained often of weariness, and would nestle close to her mother saying she "would rather not go out to play, please."

The illness was slight at first, and hope was always stirring in Mrs. Bird's heart. "Carol will feel stronger in the summertime," she would say. Or "Carol will be better when she has spent a year in the country"; or "She will outgrow it"; or "We will try a new physician."

But slowly it became plain even to Mrs. Bird

that no physician on earth could make Carol strong again; and that no "summertime" nor "country air," unless it was the everlasting summertime in a heavenly country, could bring the little girl back to health.

The cheeks and lips that were once as red as holly berries faded to faint pink; the starlike eyes grew softer, for they often gleamed through tears; and the gay child-laugh, that had been like a chime of Christmas bells, gave place to a smile so lovely, so touching, so tender and patient, that it filled the very house with a gentle radiance.

The love they all felt for her could do nothing. And when we have said that we have said all, for love is stronger than anything else in the world. Mr. and Mrs. Bird were talking it over one evening when all the children were asleep. A famous physician had visited them that day, and told them that some time, it might be in one year, it might be in more, Carol would slip quietly off forever.

"It is no use for us to shut our eyes to it any longer," said Mr. Bird, as he paced up and down the library floor. "Carol will never be well again. It seems as if I could not bear it when I think of that loveliest child doomed to lie there day after day, and, what is more, to suffer pain that we are helpless to keep away from her. Merry Christmas, indeed! It gets to be the saddest day in the year to me!"

And poor Mr. Bird sank into a chair by the table, and buried his face in his hands to keep his wife from seeing the tears that would come in spite of all his efforts.

"But, Donald, dear," said Mrs. Bird, in a trembling voice, "Christmas Day may not be so merry with us as it used to be, but it is a happy and blessed day even so, and that is almost better. I suffer for Carol's sake, but I have almost given up being sorrowful for my own. I am too happy in the child, and I see so clearly what she has done for us and the other children. Donald and Paul and Hugh were three strong, willful, boisterous boys. But now you seldom see such tenderness, devotion, thought for others, and self-denial in boys of their years. A quarrel or a hot word is almost unknown in this house. Why? Because Carol would hear it and it would distress her, she is so full of love and goodness. What's more, the boys study as hard as they can. Why? Partly, at least, because they like to teach Carol, and amuse her by telling her what they read. Everyone loves to be in Carol's room, because there they can forget their own troubles. And as for me, Donald, I am a better woman every day for Carol's sake. I have to be her strength, her hope; and she, my own little child, is my example!"

"I was wrong, dear heart," said Mr. Bird more cheerfully. "We will try not to sorrow, but to rejoice instead, that we have an 'angel of the house' like Carol."

"And as for her future," Mrs. Bird went on, "I think we need not be overanxious. I feel as if she did not belong altogether to us, but that when she has done what God sent her for, He will take her back to Himself — and it may not be very long!" Here it was poor Mrs. Bird's turn to break down, and Mr. Bird's turn to comfort her.

III. Bird's Nest

CAROL HERSELF knew nothing of her mother's tears nor her father's anxieties. They hid their feelings, knowing their sadness would distress her. So she lived on peacefully in the room where she was born.

But you never would have known that room. You see, Mr. Bird had a great deal of money. And though he felt sometimes as if he wanted to throw it all in the ocean, since it could not buy a strong body for his little girl, still he was glad that he could use his money to make the place Carol lived in just as beautiful as it could be.

The room had been extended by building a large addition that hung out over the garden below. It was a kind of sun porch, and it was so filled with windows and plants that it might have been a greenhouse. The ones on the side were even nearer the little church next door than they used to be. Those in front looked out on the beautiful harbor. And although those in the back commanded a view of nothing more than a little alley, nevertheless, they were pleasantest of all for the Ruggles family lived in a house in that alley, and the nine Ruggles children were a source of endless interest to Carol.

The window shutters could all be opened and Carol could take a real sun bath in this lovely glass house, or they could all be closed when her head ached or her eyes were tired. The carpet was a soft gray, with clusters of green bay and holly leaves. The furniture was painted white, and on each piece an artist had painted snow scenes and ringing bells and singing carols.

Donald had made a polished shelf and screwed it on the outside of the footboard of the bed, and the boys always kept this full of blooming plants, which they changed from time to time. The headboard, too, had a bracket on either side, where there were pots of maidenhair ferns.

In the windows were golden cages in which lovebirds and canaries sang. They, poor caged things, could hop as far from their wooden perches as Carol could venture from her little white bed.

On one side of the room was a bookcase filled with hundreds — yes, I mean it — with hundreds of books; books with gay-colored pictures, books without; books with black and white sketches, books with none at all; books with verses, books with stories; books that made children laugh, and some that made them cry; books with words of one syllable for tiny boys and girls, and books with words of fearful length to puzzle wise ones.

This was Carol's "circulating library." Every Saturday she chose ten books, jotting their names down in a little diary. Into these books she slipped cards that said: "Please keep this book two weeks and read it. With love, Carol Bird."

Then Mrs. Bird stepped into her carriage and took the ten books to the Children's Hospital, and brought home ten others that she had left there the fortnight before.

These books were a source of great happiness; for some of the Hospital children that were old enough to print or write, and were strong enough to do it, wrote Carol sweet little letters about the books, and she answered them, and they grew to be friends. (You do not always have to see people to love them.)

There was a shoulder-high wood ledge about the room, and on top of this, in a narrow gilt framework, ran a row of illuminated pictures, illustrating fairy tales, all in dull blue and gold and scarlet and silver. From the door to the closet there was the story of "The Fair One with Golden Locks"; from closet to bookcase, ran "Puss in Boots"; from bookcase to fireplace, was "Jack the Giant-killer"; and on the other side of the room were "Hop o' my Thumb," "The Sleeping Beauty," and "Cinderella."

Then there was a great closet full of beautiful things to wear, but they were all dressing gowns and slippers and shawls; and there were drawers full of toys and games, but they were such as you could play with on your lap. There were no skates nor balls, nor bean bags, nor tennis rackets; but, after all, other children needed these more than Carol Bird, for she was always happy and contented, whatever she had or whatever she lacked; and on her eighth Christmas after the room had been made so lovely for her, she called herself, in fun, a "bird of paradise."

On these particular December days she was happier than usual, for Uncle Jack was coming from Europe to spend the holidays. Dear, funny, jolly, loving, wise Uncle Jack, who came every two or three years, and brought so much joy with him that the world looked as black as a thunder-cloud for a week after he went away again.

The mail had brought this letter:

London, Nov. 28th, 188-.

Wish you merry Christmas, you dearest birdlings in America! Preen your feathers, and stretch the Birds' Nest a little, if you please, and let Uncle Jack in for the holidays. I am coming with such a trunk full of treasures that you'll have to borrow the stockings of a giant and giantess; I am coming to squeeze a certain little lady bird until she cries for mercy; I am coming to see if I can find a boy to take care of a little black pony that I bought lately. It's the strangest thing I ever knew; I've hunted all over Europe, and can't find a boy to suit me! I'll tell you why. I've set my heart on finding one with a dimple in his chin, because this pony particularly likes dimples! ["Hurrah!" cried Hugh. "I'll never be ashamed of my dimple again."]

Please drop a note to the clerk of the weather, and have a good, rousing snow-storm — say on the twenty-second. None of your meek, gentle, nonsensical, shilly-shally-ing snowstorms; not the sort where the flakes float lazily down from the sky as if they didn't care whether they ever got here or not and then melt away as soon as they touch the earth, but a regular, businesslike, whiz-ing, whirring, blurring, cutting snowstorm, warranted to freeze and stay on!

I should like rather a LARGE Christmas tree. We can cut a hole in the roof if the tree chances to be too high for the room.

Tell Bridget to begin to fatten a turkey, and tell her that the pudding must be unu-sually huge and darkly, deeply, lugubriously blue in color. It must be stuck so full of plums that the pudding itself will ooze out into the pan and not be brought on to the table at all. I expect to be there by the twentieth to manage these things myself, but give you these instructions in case I should be delayed.

And Carol must plead for the snowstorm — the "clerk of the weather" may pay some attention to her as she is a Christ-mas child. And she must look up the boy with the dimple for me — she's likelier to find him than I am, this minute. She must advise about the turkey, and Bridget must bring the pudding to her bedside and let her drop every separate plum into it and stir it once for luck, or I'll not eat a single slice — for Carol is the dearest part of Christmas to Uncle Jack, and he'll have none of it without her. She is better than all the turkeys and puddings and apples and spareribs and wreaths and garlands and mistletoe and stockings and chimneys and sleigh bells in the world. She is the very sweetest Christmas Carol that was ever written, said, sung, or chanted, and I am coming, as fast as ships and railway trains can carry me, to tell her so.

Carol's joy knew no bounds. Mr. and Mrs. Bird laughed and kissed each other in delight, and when the boys heard it they whooped for joy, until the Ruggles family, whose back yard joined their garden, gathered at the gate and wondered what was up in the big house.

IV. *"Bird's of a Feather Flock Together"*

UNCLE JACK really did come on the twentieth. He was not detained by business, nor did he get left behind nor snowed up, as frequently happens in stories, and in real life, too. The snowstorm came also; and the turkey. Donald came, too — Donald, with a line of down upon his upper lip, and stores of knowledge in his handsome head, and stories! You couldn't turn over a page without reminding Donald of something that happened "at college." One or the other was always at Carol's bedside, for they fancied her paler than she used to be, and they could not bear her out of sight. It was Uncle Jack, though, who sat beside her in the winter twilights. The room was quiet, and almost dark, save for the snowlight outside, and the flickering flame of the fire, that danced over the "Sleeping Beauty's" face and touched the golden locks with ruddier glory. Carol's hand, all too thin and white these days, lay close clasped in Uncle Jack's, and they talked together quietly of many, many things.

"I want to tell you all about my plans for Christmas this year, Uncle Jack," said Carol, on the first evening of his visit, "because it will be the loveliest one I ever had. The boys laugh at me for caring so much about it. But it isn't altogether because it is Christmas nor because it is my birthday. Long, long ago, when I first began to be ill, I used to think, the first thing when I waked on Christmas morning, 'Today is Christ's birthday — and mine!' And so I do not quite feel about Christmas as other girls do. Mamma says she supposes that ever so many other children have been born on that day. I often wonder where they are, Uncle Jack, and whether it is a dear thought to them, too, or whether I am so much in bed, and so often alone, that it means more to me. Oh, I do hope that none of them are poor, or cold, or hungry; and I wish, I wish they were all as happy as I, because they are really my brothers and sisters. Now, Uncle Jack dear, I am going to try and make somebody happy every single Christmas that I live, and this year it is to be the 'Ruggleses in the rear.' "

"That large and interesting brood of children in the little house at the end of the back garden?"

"Yes. Isn't it nice to see so many together? And, Uncle Jack, why do the big families always seem to live in the little houses, and the little families in the big houses? We ought to call them the Ruggles children, of course; but Donald began talking of them as the 'Ruggleses in the rear,' and Papa and Mamma took it up, and now we cannot seem to help it.

"When they first moved in, I used to sit in my window and watch them play in their back yard; they are so strong, and jolly, and good-natured — and then, one day, I had a terrible headache, and Donald asked them if they would please not scream quite so loud, and they explained that they were having a game of circus, but that they would change and play 'Deaf and Dumb' all the afternoon."

Uncle Jack smiled, "An obliging family, to be sure."

"Yes, we all thought it very kind, and I smiled at them from the window when I was well enough to be up again. Now Sarah Maud comes to her door when the children come home from school, and if Mamma nods her head, 'Yes,' that means 'Carol is very well,' and then you ought to hear the little Ruggleses yell — I believe they try to see how much noise they can make; but if Mamma shakes her head, they always play at quiet games. Then, one day, Cary, my pet canary, flew out of her cage, and Peter Ruggles caught her and brought her back, and he came up here in my room so that I could thank him."

"Is Peter the oldest?"

"No. Sarah Maud is the oldest — she helps do the washing; and Peter is the next. He is a delivery boy."

"And which is the pretty little red-haired girl?"

"That's Kitty."

"And the fat youngster?"

"Baby Larry."

"And that — most — freckled one?"

"Now, don't laugh — that's Peoria."

"Carol, you are joking."

"No, really, Uncle dear. She was born in Peoria; that's all."

"And is the next boy Oshkosh?"

"No," laughed Carol. "The others are Susan, and Clement, and Eily, and Cornelius. They all look pretty much alike except that some have more freckles than the others."

"How did you ever learn all their names?"

"Well, I have what I call a 'window school.' It

is too cold now, but in warm weather I am wheeled out on my little balcony, and the Ruggleses climb up and walk along our garden fence, and sit down on the roof of our carriage house. That brings them quite near, and I read to them and tell them stories. On Thanksgiving Day they came up for a few minutes — it was quite warm at eleven o'clock — and we told each other what we had to be thankful for. But they gave such queer answers that I couldn't understand them very well. Susan was thankful for trunks of all things in the world; Cornelius, for the horse-car; Kitty, for pork steak; and Clem, who is very quiet, brightened up when I came to him, and said he was thankful for his *lame puppy*. Wasn't that strange?"

"It might teach some of us a lesson, mightn't it, little girl?"

"That's what Mamma said. Now I'm going to give this whole Christmas to the Ruggleses. And, Uncle Jack, I earned part of the money myself."

"You, my bird! How?"

"Well, you see, it could not be my own, own Christmas if Papa gave me all the money, and I decided that I should do something on my very own; and so I talked with Mamma. Of course she thought of something lovely — she always does.

Mamma's head is just brimming over with lovely thoughts — all I have to do is ask, and out pops the very one I want. This thought was to let her write down, just as I told her, a description of how a little girl lived in her own room for three years, and what she did to amuse herself. And we sent it to a magazine and got twenty-five dollars for it. Just think!"

"Well, well," cried Uncle Jack, "my little girl is a real author! And what are you going to do with this wonderful 'own' money of yours?"

"I shall give the nine Ruggleses a grand Christmas dinner here in this very room — that will be Papa's contribution — and afterward a beautiful Christmas tree, fairly blooming with presents — that will be my part; for I have another way of adding to my twenty-five dollars so that I can buy everything I like. I should like it very much if you would sit at the head of the table, Uncle Jack, for nobody could ever be frightened of you. Mamma is going to help us, but Papa and the boys are going to eat together downstairs for fear of making the little Ruggleses shy. And after we've had a merry time with the tree and presents, we can open my window and listen to the music at the church if it comes before the children go. I have written a letter to the organist, and asked him if I might have the two songs I like best. Will you see if it is all right?

Birds' Nest, Dec. 21st, 188-.
Dear Mr. Wilkie,

I am the sick girl who lives next door to the church, and, as I seldom go out, the music on practice days and Sundays is one of my greatest pleasures.

I want to know if you can have "Carol, brothers, carol," on Christmas night, and if the boy who sings, "My ain countree" so beautifully may please sing that too. I think it is the loveliest thing in the world, but it always makes me cry; doesn't it you?

If it isn't too much trouble, I hope they can sing them both quite early, as after ten o'clock I may be asleep.

Yours respectfully,
CAROL BIRD.

P.S. — The reason I like "Carol, brothers, carol," is because the choirboys sang it eleven years ago, the morning I was born, and put it into Mamma's head to call me Carol. She didn't remember then that my other name would be Bird, because she was half asleep, and could only think of one thing at a time. Donald says if I had been born on the Fourth of July they would have named me "Independence," or if on the twenty-second of February, "Georgina," or even "Cherry," like Cherry in "Martin Chuzzlewit"; but I like my own name and birthday best.

Yours truly,
CAROL BIRD.

Uncle Jack thought the letter quite right, and did not even smile at her telling the organist so many family items.

The days flew by as they always fly in holiday time, and it was Christmas Eve before anybody knew it. The family festival was quiet and very pleasant, but almost overshadowed by the grander preparations for the next day. Carol and her pretty German nurse, Elfrida, had ransacked books, and introduced so many plans, and plays, and customs, and merry-makings from Germany, and Holland, and England, and a dozen other countries, that you would scarcely have known how or where you were keeping Christmas.

Elfrida had scattered handfuls of seed over the snow in the garden, that the wild birds might have a comfortable breakfast the next morning, and had stuffed bundles of dry grasses in the fireplaces, so that the reindeer of Santa Claus could refresh themselves after their long gallops across country. This was really done only for fun, but it pleased Carol.

And when, after dinner, the whole family had gone to church to see the Christmas decorations, Carol limped out on her crutches, and with Elfrida's help, placed all the family shoes in a row in the upper hall. That was to keep the dear ones from quarreling all through the year. There were Papa's heavy shoes; Mamma's pretty slippers next; then Uncle Jack's, Donald's, Paul's, and Hugh's. And at the end of the line her own white woolly slippers. Last, and sweetest of all, like the little children in Austria, she put a lighted candle in her window to guide the dear Christ child, lest He should stumble in the dark night as He passed up the deserted street. That done, she dropped into bed, a rather tired, but very happy Christmas fairy.

V. Some Other Birds are Taught to Fly

BEFORE THE earliest Ruggles could wake and toot his five-cent tin horn, Mrs. Ruggles was up and stirring about the house, for it was a gala day in the family. Were not all her nine children invited to a dinner party at the Birds' great house? She had been preparing for this grand occasion ever since the receipt of the invitation, which now was in an old photograph frame and hanging under the looking-glass in the most prominent place in the kitchen, where any visitor would see it.

Birds' Nest, Dec. 17th, 188-.

Dear Mrs. Ruggles,

I am going to have a dinner party on Christmas Day, and would like to have all your children come. I want everyone, please, from Sarah Maud to Baby Larry. Mamma says dinner will be at half past five, and the Christmas tree at seven; so you may expect them home at nine o'clock. Wishing you a Merry Christmas and a Happy New Year, I am yours truly,

CAROL BIRD.

Breakfast at the Ruggles' was on the table promptly at seven o'clock, and there was very little of it, too. But it was an excellent day for short rations, though Mrs. Ruggles heaved a sigh as she reflected that the boys, with their India-rubber stomachs, would be just as hungry the day after as if they had never had gone to a dinner party at all.

As soon as the scanty meal was over, she announced the plan of action: "Now Susan, you and Kitty wash up the dishes, so I can get to cutting out Larry's new suit! I'm not satisfied with his clothes, and I thought in the night of a way to make him a dress out of my old red plaid shawl — kind of Scotch style, you know, with the fringe at the bottom.

"Eily, you go find the comb and take the snarls out of the fringe. You little boys clear out from under foot! Clem, you and Con hop into bed with Larry while I wash your underclothes; 't won't take long to dry 'em. . . . Yes, I know it's bother-some, but you can't go into society 'thout taking some trouble, and anyhow I couldn't get round to 'em last night. . . . Sarah Maud, I think 't would be perfectly handsome if you ripped them brass buttons off your uncle's policeman's coat and sewed 'em in a row up the front of your green skirt. Susan, you must iron out yours and Kitty's aprons; and there, I come mighty near forgetting Peory's stockings! I counted the whole lot last night when I was washing 'em, and there ain't but nineteen anyhow you fix 'em, and no nine pairs mates nohow; and I'm not going to have my children wear odd stockings to a company dinner, fetched up as I was! — Eily, you run out and ask Mrs. Cullen to lend me a pair of stockings for Peory, and tell her if she will, Peory'll give Jim half her candy when she gets home. Won't you, Peory?"

Peoria set up a deafening howl at the idea of this projected bargain — a howl so rebellious that her mother started in her direction with flashing eye and uplifted hand; but Mrs. Ruggles let it fall suddenly, saying, "No, I vow I won't hit you Christmas Day, if you drive me crazy. But speak up smart, now, and say whether you'd rather give Jim Cullen half your candy or go bare-legged to the party?"

The matter being put so plainly, Peoria still sniffling, dried her tears, and chose the lesser evil, Clem having hastened the decision by an affectionate wink, that meant he'd go halves with her on his candy.

"That's a lady!" cried her mother. "Now, you young ones that aren't doing anything, play all you want to before noontime, and after you get through eating at twelve o'clock me and Sarah Maud's going to give you sech a washing and combing and dressing as you never had before and never will again likely, and then I'm going to set you down and give you two solid hour's training in manners; and 't won't be no fooling neither."

"All we've got to do's go eat!" grumbled Peter.

"Well, that's enough," responded his mother, "there's more 'n one way of eating, let me tell you, and you've got a heap to learn about it, Peter Ruggles. Land sakes, I wish you children could see the way I was fetched up to eat. I never took a meal in the kitchen before I married Ruggles; but you can't keep up that style with nine young ones 'n' your Pa always off to sea."

The big Ruggleses worked so well, and the little Ruggleses kept from "under foot" so successfully, that by one o'clock nine complete outfits were carefully laid out on the beds.

"Now, Sarah Maud," said Mrs. Ruggles, her face shining with excitement, "we can begin. I've got a boiler and a kettle and a pot of hot water. Peter, you go into the back bedroom, and I'll take Susan, Kitty, Peory, and Cornelius; and Sarah Maud, you take Clem and Eily and Larry, one at a time. Scrub 'em and rinse 'em, or at any rate get as far as you can with 'em, and then I'll finish 'em while you do yourself."

Sarah Maud couldn't have scrubbed with any more decision and force if she had been doing floors, and the little Ruggleses bore it bravely, not from natural heroism, but for the joy that was set before them. And when the clock struck four they were all clothed, and most of them in their right minds, ready for those last touches that always take the most time.

Kitty's red hair was curled in thirty-four ringlets, Sarah Maud's was braided in one pig-tail, and Susan's, Eily's, and Peoria's, in two braids apiece. Then, exciting moment, came linen collars for some and neckties and bows for others — a magnificent green glass pin was sewed into Peter's purple necktie — and Eureka! the Ruggleses were dressed!

A row of seats was then formed directly

through the middle of the kitchen. There were not quite chairs enough for ten, since the family had rarely wanted to sit down all at once, somebody's always being out, or in bed, but the wood-box and the coal-hod finished out the line nicely. The children took their places according to age, Sarah Maud at the head and Larry on a board laid across the coal-hod, and Mrs. Ruggles seated herself in front, surveying them proudly as she wiped the sweat of honest toil from her brow.

"Well," she exclaimed, "if I do say so as I shouldn't, I never have seen a cleaner, more stylish mess of children in my life! I do wish Ruggles could look at you for a minute! — Larry Ruggles, how many times have I got to tell you not to keep pulling at your sash? Haven't I told you if it comes untied your top and bottom will part company in

the middle, and then where'll you be? — Now look
me in the eye, all of you! I've often told you what
kind of a family the McGrills were. I've got reason
to be proud, goodness knows! Your uncle is on the
police force of New York City; you can take up
the paper most any day and see his name printed
out — James McGrill — and I can't have my children fetched up common, like some folks'; when
they go out they've got to have clothes, and learn
to act decent! Now I want to see how you're going
to behave when you get there tonight. Let's start
in at the beginning and act out the whole business.
Pile into the bedroom, there, every last one of you
and show me how you're going to go into the
parlor. This'll be the parlor, and I'll be Mrs.
Bird."

The youngsters hustled into the next room in

high glee, and Mrs. Ruggles drew herself up in the chair with haughty expression that was not at all like modest Mrs. Bird.

In the small bedroom there was such a clatter that you would have thought a herd of wild cattle had broken loose. The door opened, and they straggled in, all the little ones giggling, with Sarah Maud at the head, looking as if she had been caught in the act of stealing sheep; while Larry, being last in line, seemed to think the door a sort of gate to heaven which would be shut in his face if he didn't get there in time; accordingly he struggled ahead of his elders and disgraced himself by tumbling in head foremost.

Mrs. Ruggles looked severe. "There, I knew you'd do it some such fool way! Now go in there and try it over again, every last one of you, and if Larry can't come in on two legs he can stay home — d' you hear?"

The matter began to assume a graver aspect. The little Ruggleses stopped giggling and backed into the bedroom, issuing presently with lock step, Indian file, a scared and hunted expression on every face.

"No, no, no!" cried Mrs. Ruggles, in despair. "That's worse yet; you look for all the world like a gang of pris'ners! There isn't any style to that.

Spread out more, can't you, and act kind of careless like — nobody's goin' ter kill you!" The third time brought deserved success, and the pupils took their seats in the row. "Now, you know," said Mrs. Ruggles impressively, "there aren't enough decent hats to go round, and if there were I don't know as I'd let you wear 'em, for the boys would never think to take 'em off when they got inside — but anyhow, there aren't enough good ones. Now, look me in the eye. You needn't wear any hats, none of you, and when you get into the parlor, and they ask you to lay off your hats, Sarah Maud must speak up and say it was such a pleasant evening and such a short walk that you left your hats at home to save trouble. Now, can you remember?"

All the little Ruggleses shouted, "Yes, ma'am!" in chorus.

"What have *you* got to do with it?" demanded their mother; "did I tell *you* to say it? Wasn't I talkin' to Sarah Maud?"

The little Ruggleses hung their heads. "Yes, ma'am," they piped, more feebly.

"Now get up, all of you, and try it. Speak up, Sarah Maud."

Sarah Maud's tongue clove to the roof of her mouth.

"Quick!"

"Ma thought — it was — such a pleasant hat that we'd — we'd better leave our short walk to home," recited Sarah Maud, in an agony of mental effort.

This was too much for the boys. An earthquake of suppressed giggles swept all along the line.

"Oh, whatever shall I do with you?" moaned the unhappy mother; "I s'pose I've got to teach it to you!" — which she did, word for word, until Sarah Maud thought she could stand on her head and say it backward.

"Now Cornelius, what are *you* going to say to make yourself good company?"

"Me? Dunno!" said Cornelius, turning pale.

"Well, you ain't going to sit there like a bump on a log without saying a word to pay for your vittles, are you? Ask Mrs. Bird how she's feelin' this evening, or if Mr. Bird's having a busy season, or how this kind of weather agrees with him, or somethin' like that — Now we'll make believe we've got to the dinner — that won't be so hard, 'cause you'll have something to do — it's awful bothersome to stand round an act stylish. If they have napkins, Sarah Maud down to Peory may put 'em in their laps, and the rest of you can tuck 'em in your necks. Don't eat with your fingers — don't grab no vittles off one another's plates; don't reach out for nothing, but wait till you're asked, and if you never get asked don't get up and grab it . . . Don't spill nothing on the tablecloth, or like as not Mrs. Bird'll send you away from the table — and I hope she will if you do!

"Now we'll try a few things to see how they'll go! Mr. Clement, do you eat cranberry sauce?"

"Bet your life!" cried Clem, who in the excitement of the moment had not taken in the idea exactly and had mistaken this for an ordinary bosom-of-the-family question.

"Clement McGrill Ruggles, do you mean to tell me that you'd say that at a dinner party? I'll give you one more chance. Mr. Clement, will you take some of the cranberry?"

"Yes ma'am, thank you kindly, if you happen to have any handy."

"Very good, indeed! But they won't give you two tries tonight, you just remember that! — Miss Peory, do you speak for white or dark meat?"

"I'm not partic'lar — anything that nobody else wants, will suit me," answered Peory with her best air.

"First rate! Nobody could speak more genteel than that. Miss Kitty, will you have hard or soft sauce with your pudding?"

"Hard or soft? Oh! A little of both, if you please, and I'm much obliged," said Kitty, bowing with decided ease and grace; at which all the other Ruggleses pointed the finger of shame at her, and Peter grunted expressively, that their meaning might not be mistaken.

"You just stop your grunting, Peter Ruggles; that wasn't greedy, that was all right. I wish I could get it into your heads that it ain't so much what you say, as the way you say it. Eily, you and Larry are too little to train, so you just look at the rest, and do's they do, and the Lord have mercy on you and help you to act decent! Now, is there anything more you'd like to practice?"

"If you tell me one more thing, I can't set up and eat," said Peter, gloomily; "I'm so cram full of manners now I'm ready to bust, without no dinner at all."

"Me too," chimed in Cornelius.

"Well, I'm sorry for you both," rejoined Mrs. Ruggles, sarcastically; "if the amount of manners you've got on hand now troubles you, you're dreadful easy hurt! Now, Sarah Maud, after

dinner, you must get up and say, 'I guess we'd better be going'; and if they say, 'Oh, no, sit a while longer,' you can sit; but if they don't say anything, you've got to get up and go. . . . Now have you got that into your head?"

"Well," answered Sarah Maud, mournfully, "seems as if this whole dinner party set right square on top of me! Maybe I could manage my own manners, but to manage nine mannerses is worse'n staying to home!"

"Oh, don't fret," said her mother, good-naturedly, "I guess you'll get along. I wouldn't mind if folks would only say, 'Oh, children will be children'; but they won't. They'll say, 'Land 'o goodness, who fetched them children up?' Now it's quarter past five, and you can go now. Remember about the hats, don't all talk ter once, and Susan, lend your handkerchief to Peory. Peter, don't keep wiggling yer tiepin. Cornelius, hold your head up straight — Sarah Maud, don't take your eyes off Larry, and Larry you keep hold of Sarah Maud and do just as she says — and whatever you do, all of you never forget for one second that your mother was a McGrill."

VI. "When the Pie Was Opened The Birds Began to Sing!"

THE CHILDREN went out of the back door quietly, and were presently lost to sight, Sarah Maud slipping and stumbling along absent-mindedly, as she recited rapidly under her breath, "Itwassuch apleasantevenin' n' suchashortwalk,thatwethought we'dleaveourhatstohome."

Peter rang the doorbell, and presently a servant admitted them, and, whispering something in Sarah's ear, drew her downstairs into the kitchen. The other Ruggleses stood in horror-stricken groups as the door closed behind their commanding officer; but there was no time for reflection, for a voice from above was heard, saying, "Come right upstairs please!"

Accordingly, they walked upstairs, and Elfrida, the nurse, ushered them into a room more splendid than anything they had ever seen. But, oh woe! Where was Sarah Maud? And was it Fate that Mrs. Bird should say, at once, "Did you lay your hats in the hall?" Peter felt himself elected by circumstance the head of the family, and, casting one imploring look at tongue-tied Susan, standing next him, said huskily, "It was so very pleasant — that — that —" "That we hadn't good hats enough to go round," put in little Susan bravely, to help him out, and then froze with horror that the ill-fated words had slipped off her tongue.

However, Mrs. Bird said, pleasantly, "Of course you wouldn't wear hats such a short distance — I forgot when I asked. Now will you come right in to Miss Carol's room? She is so anxious to see you."

Just then Sarah Maud came up the backstairs, so radiant with joy from her secret interview with the cook that Peter could have pinched her with a clear conscience, and Carol gave them a joyful welcome. "But where is Baby Larry?" she cried, looking over the group with searching eye. "Didn't he come?"

"Larry! Larry!" Good gracious, where was Larry? They were all sure that he had come in with them, for Susan said she remembered scolding him for tripping over the doormat. Uncle Jack laughed. "Are you sure there were nine of you?" he asked, jokingly.

"I think so, sir," said Peoria, timidly, "but anyhow, there was Larry," and she showed signs of weeping.

"Oh, well, cheer up!" cried Uncle Jack. "I guess he's not lost — only mislaid. I'll go and find him before you can say Jack Robinson!"

"I'll go, too, if you please, sir," said Sarah Maud, "for it was my place to mind him, an' if he's lost I can't relish my vittles!"

The other Ruggleses stood rooted to the floor. If this was a dinner party, why were such things ever spoken of as festive occasions?

Sarah Maud went out through the hall, calling, "Larry! Larry!" and without any interval of suspense a little voice piped up from below, "Here I be!"

The truth was that Larry, being deserted by his natural guardian, dropped behind the rest, and wriggled into the hat tree to wait for her, having no notion of walking unprotected into the jaws of a dinner party. Finding that she did not come, he tried to crawl from his refuge and call somebody, when — dark and dreadful ending to a tragic day — he found that he was too much intertwined with umbrellas and canes to move a single step. He was afraid to yell, but the sound of Sarah Maud's familiar voice, some seconds later, carried him upstairs, and soon had him in breathless fits of laughter, while Carol so made the other Ruggleses forget themselves that they were presently talking like accomplished diners-out.

Carol's bed had been moved into the farthest corner of the room, and she was propped up on it, dressed in a wonderful soft white robe. Her golden hair fell in fluffy curls over her white forehead and neck, her cheeks flushed delicately, her eyes beamed with joy, and the children told their mother afterward that she looked as beautiful as the angels in the picture books.

There was a great bustle behind a huge screen in another part of the room, and at half past five this was taken away, and the Christmas dinner table stood revealed. What a wonderful sight it was to the Ruggles children! It blazed with tall, colored candles, it gleamed with glass and silver, it blushed with flowers, it groaned with good things to eat. So it was not strange that the Ruggleses, forgetting that their mother was a McGrill, shrieked in admiration of the fairy spectacle. But Larry's behavior was the most disgraceful, for he went at once to a high chair, climbed up like a squirrel, gave a look at the turkey, clapped his hands in ecstasy, rested his fat arms on the table, and cried with joy, "I beat the hull lot o'yer!" Carol laughed until she cried, giving orders meanwhile — "Uncle Jack, please sit at the head, Sarah Maud at the foot, and that will leave four on each side. Mamma is going to help Elfrida, so you will not have to look after each other, but just have a good time."

A sprig of holly lay by each plate, and nothing would do but each little Ruggles must leave his seat and have it pinned on by Carol, and as each course was served, one of them pleaded to take something to her. There was hurrying to and fro, for it is quite a difficult matter to serve a Christmas dinner so far away from the downstairs kitchen. But if it had been necessary to carry every dish up a rope ladder the servants would gladly have done so — both for Carol's sake, and the joy and gusto with which the Ruggles children ate up the food. There were turkey and chicken, with delicious gravy and stuffing, and there were half a dozen vegetables, with cranberry jelly, and celery, and pickles; and as for the elegant way in which these delicacies were served, the Ruggleses never forgot it as long as they lived.

Peter nudged Kitty, who sat next him, and said, "Look! Every feller's got his own partic'lar butter; I s'pose that's to show you can eat that and no more. No, it ain't either, for that pig of a Peory's just getting another helping!"

"Yes," whispered Kitty, "and the napkins are marked with big red letters! I wonder if that's so nobody'll nip 'em; an' oh, Peter, look at the pictures sticking right on to the dishes! Did you *ever*?"

"The plums is all took out o'my cramb'ry sauce an' it's friz to a stiff jell," whispered Peoria, in wild excitement.

"Hi — yah! I got a wishbone!" sang Larry, regardless of Sarah Maud's frown. She asked to

have his seat changed, giving as excuse that he generally sat beside her, and would "feel strange"; the true reason was that she desired to kick him gently, under the table, whenever he passed beyond what might be termed "the McGrill line."

"I declare to goodness," murmured Susan, on the other side, "there's so much to look at I can't scarcely eat anything!"

"Bet your life I can!" said Peter, who had kept one servant busily employed ever since he sat down; for, luckily, no one was asked by Uncle Jack whether he would have a second helping, but the dishes were quietly passed under their noses again and again, and not a single Ruggles refused anything that was offered.

Then, when Carol and Uncle Jack saw that more turkey was a physical impossibility, the dessert was brought in — a dessert that would have frightened a strong man after such a dinner as had preceded it! Not so the Ruggleses!

There were plum pudding, mince pie, and ice cream; and there were nuts, and raisins, and oranges. Kitty chose ice cream, explaining that she knew it "by sight, though she hadn't ever tasted any"; but all the rest took the entire variety, without any regard to consequences.

"My dear child," whispered Uncle Jack, as he took Carol an orange, "there is no doubt about the necessity of this feast, but I do advise you after this to have them twice a year, or quarterly perhaps, for the way these children eat is positively dangerous; I assure you I tremble for that terrible Peoria. I'm going to run races with her after dinner."

"Never mind," laughed Carol; "let them have enough for once; and I shall invite them oftener next year."

The feast being over, the Ruggleses leaned back in their chairs and the table was cleared in a trice. Then a door was opened into the next room, and there, in a corner facing Carol's bed, which had been wheeled as close as possible, stood the brilliantly lighted Christmas tree, glittering with gilded walnuts and tiny silver balloons, and wreathed with snowy chains of popcorn. The presents had been bought mostly with Carol's story money, and were selected after long consultations with Mrs. Bird. Each girl had a blue knitted hood, and each boy a red crocheted scarf, all made by Mamma, Carol, and Elfrida. Then every girl had a pretty plaid dress of a different color, and every boy a warm coat of the right size.

Here the useful presents stopped. Carol had pleaded to give them something "for fun." "I know they need clothes," she had said, when they were talking over the matter just after Thanksgiving, "but they don't care much for them, after all. Now, Papa, won't you *please* give me the money you would spend on presents for me, so that I can buy presents for the Ruggleses?"

"You can have both," said Mr. Bird promptly. "Is there any need of my little girl's going without her own Christmas, I should like to know? Spend all the money you like."

"But that isn't the thing," objected Carol, nestling close to her father. "The presents wouldn't really be from me, then, and haven't I almost everything already? I'm the happiest girl in the world this year, with Uncle Jack and Donald at home. Why won't you let me do it? You never look half as happy when you are getting your presents as when you are giving us ours. Now, Papa, say 'yes,' or I shall have to be very firm and disagreeable with you!"

"Very well, Your Highness, I surrender. But a bronze figure of Santa Claus, and in the little round belly that shakes when he laughs like a bowl of jelly,' is a wonderful clock — oh, you would never give it up if you could see it!"

"Nonsense," laughed Carol. "As I never have to get up to breakfast, nor go to bed, nor catch trains, I think my old clock will do very well! Now, Mamma, what were you going to give me?"

"Oh, I hadn't decided. A few more books, and a gold thimble, and a smelling bottle, and a music box, perhaps."

"Poor Carol," laughed the child, merrily, "she can afford to give up these lovely things, for there will still be left Uncle Jack, and Donald, and Paul, and Hugh, and Uncle Rob, and Aunt Elsie, and a dozen other people to fill her Christmas stocking!"

So Carol had her way, as she generally did, and Sarah Maud had a set of Louisa May Alcott's books, and Peter a modest silver watch, Cornelius a tool chest, Clement a doghouse for his lame puppy, Larry a magnificent Noah's ark, and each of the little girls a beautiful doll.

You can well believe that everybody was very merry! All the family, from Mr. Bird down to the cook, said that they had never seen so much happiness in the space of three hours! But it had to end, as all things do. The candles flickered and went out. The tree shorn of gifts was left alone with just its gilded ornaments. Mrs. Bird had Elfrida lead the children downstairs at half past eight, thinking that Carol looked tired.

"Now, my darling, you have done quite enough for one day," said Mrs. Bird, getting Carol into her nightgown. "If you were to feel worse tomorrow that would be a sad ending to such a charming evening."

"Oh, wasn't it a lovely, lovely time," sighed Carol. "From first to last, everything was just right. I shall never forget Larry's face when he looked at the turkey; nor Peter's, when he saw his watch; nor that sweet, sweet Kitty's smile when she kissed her doll; nor the tears in poor Sarah Maud's eyes when she thanked me for her books; nor —"

"But we mustn't talk any longer about it tonight," said Mrs. Bird, anxiously. "You are too tired, dear."

"I am not so very tired, Mamma. I have felt well all day; not a bit of pain anywhere. Perhaps this has done me good."

"Perhaps," Mrs. Bird smiled. "It was a merry time. Now, may I close the door and leave you alone, dear? Papa and I will steal in softly by and by to see if you are all right; but I think you need to be very quiet."

"Oh, I'm willing to stay alone; but I am not sleepy yet, and I am going to hear the music, you know."

"Yes, I have opened the window a little, and put the screen in front of it, so that you won't feel a draft."

"Can I have the shutters open? And won't you turn my bed a little, please? This morning I woke ever so early, and one bright, beautiful star shone in that eastern window. I never noticed it before, and I thought of the Star in the East, that guided the wise men to the place where the baby Jesus was. Good night, Mamma. Such a happy, happy day!"

"Good night, my precious Christmas Carol — mother's own Christmas child."

"Bend your head a minute, Mother dear," whispered Carol, calling her mother back. "Mamma, dear, I do think that we have kept Christ's birthday this time just as He would like it. Don't you?"

"I am sure of it," said Mrs. Bird softly.

VII. *The Birdling Flies Away*

THE RUGGLESES had finished a last romp in the library with Paul and Hugh, and Uncle Jack had taken them home and stayed a while to chat with Mrs. Ruggles, who opened the door for them, her face all aglow with excitement and delight. When Kitty and Clem showed her the oranges and nuts that they had kept for her, she astonished them by saying that at six o'clock Mrs. Bird had sent her in the finest dinner she had ever seen in her life; and not only that, but a piece of dress goods that must have cost a dollar a yard if it cost a cent.

As Uncle Jack went down the little porch he looked back into the window for a last glimpse of the family, as the children gathered about their mother, showing their beautiful presents again and again, and then upward to a window in the great house yonder. "A little child shall lead them," he thought. "Well, if — if anything ever happens to

Carol, I will take the Ruggleses under my wing."

"Softly, Uncle Jack," whispered the boys, as he walked into the library a little while later. "We are listening to the music in the church. The choir sang 'Carol, brothers, carol,' a while ago, and now we think the organist is beginning to play 'My ain countree' for Carol."

"I hope she hears it," said Mrs. Bird, "but they are very late tonight, and she may be asleep. It is almost ten o'clock."

The boy soprano, clad in white surplice, stood in the organ loft. The light shone full upon him, and his pale face, with its serious blue eyes, looked paler than usual. Perhaps it was something in the tender trill of the voice, or in the sweet words, but there were tears in many eyes, both in the church and in the big house next door.

> "I am far frae my hame,
>   I am weary aften whiles
> For the langed-for hame-bringing',
>   An' my Faether's welcome smiles;
> An' I'll ne'er be fu' content,
>   Until my e'en do see
> The golden gates o'heaven
>   In my ain countree."

There were tears in many eyes, but not in Carol's. The "wee birdie" in the great house had flown to its "home nest." Carol had fallen asleep! The loving heart had quietly ceased to beat.

So sad an ending to a happy day! And yet Carol's mother, even in the freshness of her grief, was glad that her darling had slipped away on the loveliest day of her life, out of its glad content, into everlasting peace.

She was glad that she had gone as she had come, on the wings of song, when Christmas was brimming over with joy; glad of every grateful smile, of every joyous burst of laughter, of every loving thought and word and deed that the last day had brought.

Sadness reigned, it is true, in the little house behind the garden.

One day poor Sarah Maud, with a courage born of despair, threw on her hood and shawl, walked straight to a certain house a mile away, up the marble steps into good Dr. Bartol's office.

"Oh, sir," she cried, "it was me an' our children that went to Miss Carol's last dinner party, an' if we made her worse we can't never be happy again!" Then the kind old gentleman took her hand in his and told her to dry her tears, for neither she nor any of her flock had hastened Carol's flight — indeed, he said that had it not been for the strong hopes and wishes that filled her tired heart, Carol could not have stayed long enough to keep that last merry Christmas with her dear ones.

And so the old years, filled with memories, die, one after another, and the new years, bright with hopes, are born to take their places; but Carol lives again in every chime of Christmas bells that peal glad tidings and in every Christmas anthem sung by childish voices.

ABOUT THE AUTHOR

KATE DOUGLAS WIGGIN was born Kate Douglas Smith in Philadelphia, Pennsylvania, in 1856, and she grew up in Maine. Her first story, "Half-a-Dozen Housekeepers," was sold in 1873 to Mary Mapes Dodge at *St. Nicholas* Magazine. After moving to California Ms. Wiggin started the first free kindergarten in the West. Writing children's books became her way of funding kindergarten projects.

In 1881 she married a lawyer named Samuel Wiggin, and the two of them moved to New York City. *The Story of Patsy*, her first novel, was published in 1883. The beloved *Birds' Christmas Carol* followed four years later. Ms. Wiggin wrote more than twenty books. Her best-known work, *Rebecca of Sunnybrook Farm*, was published in 1903. Left a widow in 1889, Kate Douglas Wiggin had a second marriage, to George Christopher Riggs. She died in England at the age of sixty-six.